THE KID FROM PLANET Z

FOR AMANDA,
WHO NEVER LETS ANYONE
FEEL LIKE A STRANGER
—NK

FOR PIPO—LT

GROSSET & DUNLAP

Penguin Young Readers Group
An Imprint of Penguin Random House LLC

Penguin supports copyright. Copyright fuels creativity, encourages
diverse voices, promotes free speech, and creates a vibrant culture.
Thank you for buying an authorized edition of this book and for complying
with copyright laws by not reproducing, scanning, or distributing any part
of it in any form without permission. You are supporting writers and
allowing Penguin to continue to publish books for every reader.

Text copyright © 2017 by Nancy Krulik. Illustrations copyright
© 2017 by Penguin Random House LLC. All rights reserved.
Published by Grosset & Dunlap, an imprint of Penguin Random House LLC,
345 Hudson Street, New York, New York 10014. GROSSET & DUNLAP
is a trademark of Penguin Random House LLC. Manufactured in China.

Library of Congress Cataloging-in-Publication Data is available.

ISBN 9780451533432 (paperback)   10 9 8 7 6 5 4 3 2 1
ISBN 9780451533449 (library binding)   10 9 8 7 6 5 4 3 2 1

NANCY KRULIK

THE KID FROM PLANET Z

DON'T SNEEZE!

ILLUSTRATED BY
LOUIS THOMAS

GROSSET & DUNLAP ★ AN IMPRINT OF PENGUIN RANDOM HOUSE

GOT A TISSUE?

How do all those strange earthlings fit in that teeny tiny car?" Zeke Zander asked his friends Eddie and Amelia.

Amelia gave Zeke an odd look. "Strange *what*?" she asked.

Oops. Zeke had forgotten. Earthlings did not call themselves earthlings.

"I mean, how do all those strange *people* fit in that teeny tiny car?" he said instead.

"I don't know," Eddie said. "It's a clown trick."

Zeke watched as three more earthlings with red noses and rainbow-colored hair piled out of the car.

There was no way they could have all been in there at the same time.

But it sure looked like they were.

Sometimes the strangest things happen on Planet Earth.

"That clown just sprayed soda on the other one's head," Amelia said. "*Ha ha ha.*"

Zeke reached into his pocket and pulled out a tissue.

"Here you go," he said to Amelia.

Amelia looked at the tissue. Then she looked at Zeke.

"What's that for?" she asked him.

"For your nose," Zeke told her.

"You're a funny guy, Zeke," Amelia said.

Zeke looked at Amelia strangely. *What is so funny about a tissue?*

"Here comes the tiger trainer," Eddie said.

Zeke watched as an earthling led

three orange-and-black cats into the center ring. There were three stools waiting there.

The earthling yelled something at the giant cats.

The giant cats jumped up onto the stools.

The earthling lifted his hand.

The cats leaped up onto their hind legs.

The earthling turned his hand in a circle.

The cats danced around and around.

Wow! It looked like the earthling was in charge of the big cats.

That would *never* happen on Planet Z.

On Planet Z, the *cats* were in charge.

Of course, Zeke wasn't *on* Planet Z anymore. He was on Earth.

He'd been here since his family's spaceship had crashed. And he was stuck here until they were able to fix the ship and fly home.

Still, Earth wasn't all bad.

Earth kids played fun games like tag and hide-and-seek.

They went to great places like the circus.

And they drank sweet apple juice.

Zeke was thirsty. He pulled his juice box from his backpack.

He stuck one end of the straw through the little silver circle.

Then he stuck the other end of the straw in his ear and started to drink.

Eddie watched Zeke slurp up the apple juice. Then he let out a loud "*ha ha ha.*"

"I'm sorry," Zeke said. "I'm all out of tissues."

Eddie gave him a funny look. "Huh?" he asked.

Zeke took another sip of his apple juice.

"I love your ear trick," Eddie told him. "Someday I'm going to figure out how you make the juice disappear into there."

Zeke frowned. He hoped Eddie never figured it out. Because then he would know Zeke was a kid from Planet Z. All zeebops drank with their ears.

Zeke could never let Eddie know that he and his family came from outer space. He couldn't let *anyone* know.

Because there was no telling what horrible things might happen if information like that got into the wrong hands.

2

WHAT A JERK

I love cotton candy," Amelia said as the kids each bought a cone of the fluffy stuff at the end of the circus show.

Zeke didn't understand why it was called cotton candy. It wasn't made of cotton at all. It was made of spun sugar.

"It's like I'm biting into a cloud," Amelia said.

"No, it's not," Zeke told her. "Clouds

aren't pink. And they don't taste very sweet."

"How do you know?" Amelia asked him. "Clouds might taste sweet. We just don't know, because no one has ever eaten one."

Zeke knew. He had tried eating a cloud once. But that didn't go so well. The cloud tasted like water mixed with dirt. Which was kind of gross.

But, of course, he didn't say that.

"There's nothing yummier than cotton candy," Amelia said.

Actually, Zeke thought the paper cone around the cotton candy would taste a lot better than the pink cloud.

It lasted longer, too. Paper didn't melt in your mouth the way cotton

candy did. You had to chew it for
a long time until it got gooey enough
to swallow.

Chomp.

Zeke bit into
the paper cone at
the bottom of his
cotton candy. *Yum.*

Amelia smiled. "I love how you're
always clowning around," she told
Zeke.

"Me?" Zeke asked.

"Yeah," Amelia said. "Who else
do we know who would eat paper?"

"You better not clown around
tomorrow when we're doing our skit
in class," Eddie warned Zeke. "You
know how important it is."

Zeke nodded. He knew.

All last week, the kids at school had been writing skits based on stories from *Aesop's Fables*. The best skit in each grade was going to be chosen to be part of a big show in front of the whole school.

Eddie really wanted to be in that show. So did Amelia.

Zeke wasn't sure what was so great about being in the big show. But he wanted his friends to be happy. So he had worked really hard on their skit about "The Boy Who Cried Wolf."

"Our skit has to be perfect if we want Mr. Zimmermoon to choose us," Eddie said.

"We're going to win," Amelia said. "I know it."

She opened her mouth to take another bite of cotton candy.

But before she could, a huge hand with dirty fingernails grabbed the pink fluffy stuff away from her.

"Slade!" Amelia shouted at the boy who'd stolen her candy. "Give that back."

The big fifth-grader shoved a wad of Amelia's cotton candy into his mouth. Then he opened wide and showed Amelia his tongue.

"You want it back?" he asked Amelia. "Take it."

Amelia shook her head. "That's gross," she said.

Slade grinned and ripped the cotton candy from the cone. He thrust the cone into her hand and walked away.

"I can't believe he did that," Amelia said angrily.

"I can," Eddie said. "Slade's the nastiest kid in school."

Zeke watched as Slade grabbed a kid's box of popcorn. He ate two kernels and dumped the rest on the kid's head.

Slade sure was mean.

Mean enough to live on Planet Q—where the evil querks lurked.

Querks were jerks.

Just like Slade.

But of course Zeke couldn't tell Eddie and Amelia about the querk jerks from Planet Q. So instead, he pointed to the empty paper cone in Amelia's hand.

"You gonna eat that?" he asked.

"*Ha ha ha,*" Amelia answered.

Then Zeke let out a loud "*Ha ha ha. Ha ha ha.*"

"You are really funny," Eddie said.

Funny? Why would Eddie say that? There was nothing funny about Zeke going *ha ha ha.*

In fact, *ha ha ha* meant there was trouble brewing.

And it was brewing inside Zeke.

3

THAT'S SICK

Ha ha ha.

The next morning, Zeke was still *ha ha ha*-ing.

His mother raced into his room.

"You're sick," she said. "I heard you going *ha ha ha* all night."

Zeke knew she was right. When zeebops sneezed, the sound that came out of their noses was *ha ha ha*.

"I wonder where you could have caught a cold," his mother said.

21

Zeke thought back to yesterday. Eddie and Amelia had been going *ha ha ha* a lot. That was why Zeke had given Amelia his last tissue. He must have caught this cold from them.

"*Ha ha ha.*" Zeke sneezed again.

"That settles it," Zeke's mom said. "You better stay on your head today."

Zeke knew his mom wanted him to go back to sleep. Zeebops slept on their heads.

But Zeke couldn't go back to sleep. Not today.

"I can't," he told his mom. "We're doing our skit at school today. I can't let Eddie and Amelia down. They are my best friends. My *only* friends— at least on Earth."

Zeke felt something dripping from his eye. He wiped away a bright green tear.

"You see?" his mom told him. "You're sick. You have the flu."

That was probably true. When zeebops got the flu, they leaked green tears.

"It doesn't matter," Zeke said. "I can't stay home."

"We'll see what Zeus says about that," his mom said. She headed for the stairs.

Gulp. Zeke was worried.

Zeus was their leader. Whatever he told the Zanders to do, they did.

What if Zeus told him to stay home?

Zeke had to find a way out of there. Fast.

He wiggled his right antenna. Then he disappeared.

"Oh no you don't," his mother said. "You're not going to go invisible and sneak out of this house."

Bummer. His mom had caught him.

Zeke wiggled his left antenna.
Now his mom could see him again.

He followed his mom down the
stairs and into the yard.

Zeke's dad was already there,
working on their spaceship.

"Where's Zeus?" Zeke's mom
asked.

Zeke's dad pointed to the corner of the yard. Zeus was scratching his back against a tree trunk and muttering to himself.

Zeke's mom walked over to the cat.

"Zeus," she said. "I need you to talk some sense into Zeke. He's sick. He needs to stay home today."

"I'm not that sick," Zeke insisted. "I can go to school."

Zeus glared at both of them. "How can you bother me about a little cold? Can't you tell we're under attack?" he asked.

"What are you talking about?" Zeke asked the cat. "I don't see anyone."

"They're too small to see," Zeus said. "But they're here. Can't you hear them? They're going *pop pop pop*."

Zeke listened.

"I don't hear anything," he said.

"Maybe your ears are clogged because you're sick," Zeke's mom said.

"Can *you* hear them?" Zeke asked her.

"No," she admitted.

"Well, *I* can hear them." Zeus

scratched harder against the tree trunk. "And I can feel them. They're sticking me with tiny swords."

"Zeus," Zeke's mom said, "I need you to tell Zeke he can't go to school today."

"I have no time for this," Zeus

shouted at her. "I'm fighting an army of tiny, popping sword fighters!"

"So, I *can* go to school?" Zeke asked him.

"I don't care what you do," Zeus said. He scratched his ear. "They're attacking from all sides now!"

Hmmm . . .

Zeus hadn't said Zeke could go to school.

But he hadn't said he *couldn't* go, either.

Zeke was taking that as a yes. He hurried off before his mother could stop him.

Yay! Zeke was going to school to do his skit with Eddie and Amelia. And it was going to be awesome—

"Ha ha ha."

Or it would be, if he could keep himself from sneezing all the way through it.

"Ha ha ha."

That was a *big* if.

4

THE ZEEBOP WHO CRIED WOLF

ow, remember," Eddie whispered to Zeke at school later that day. "You gotta look really scared when I do my wolf song."

"I will," Zeke said.

"Okay," Mr. Zimmermoon told the class. "Now we're going to see a skit by Amelia, Eddie, and Zeke. Show us what you've got, kids."

Zeke and his pals walked to the front of the room.

They were all wearing special costumes.

Eddie was wearing a wolf mask.

Amelia was wearing a white woolly sweater that made her look like a sheep.

Zeke was dressed like an Earth boy. That was kind of like a costume for him.

"This is the story of 'The Boy Who Cried Wolf,'" Eddie told the class. "It's about a boy who told lies and got in a lot of trouble."

Now it was Zeke's turn to say his first line.

"I am so bored and lonely," he said. "I have no one to talk to, except the sheep."

"Sheep are fun to talk to," Amelia-the-sheep told him. "We tell great jokes. Like what do you call a sheep dressed in chocolate?"

"I don't know," Zeke answered. "What?"

"A chocolate *baaaa*," Amelia said.

A few of the kids in the class let out a little *"ha ha ha."*

Zeke wondered if they were getting sick, too.

"And where do sheep go to get their hair cut?" Amelia asked.

"I don't know," Zeke said. "Where?"

"The *baa baa* shop," Amelia told him.

"Ha ha ha." Now a whole bunch of kids seemed to be sneezing.

Amelia started to say her next line. But Zeke wasn't listening anymore. He was too busy trying to stop *his* nose from sneezing.

He shoved his finger up one nostril to keep the sneeze in.

So the sneeze moved to the other side.

Zeke's nose twitched.

It itched.

And then . . .

"Ha ha ha ha ha ha!"

A giant sneeze burst out of his nose.

Eddie and Amelia stared at him. They looked surprised.

Zeke kept sneezing. *"Ha ha ha."*
And sneezing. *"Ha ha ha."*
And sneezing. *"Ha ha ha ha ha!"*
Now everyone in the class was *ha ha ha*-ing—except Eddie and Amelia. They didn't seem to be sick like they had been yesterday.

Maybe this was just a twenty-four-hour flu.

"Okay, guys," Mr. Zimmermoon said to Eddie, Amelia, and Zeke. "That's enough. Take your seats."

Eddie pulled off his wolf mask. He looked like he was going to cry.

"But I didn't get to do my wolf song," he told Mr. Zimmermoon.

"I've been practicing it for a week. I made up a tap dance and everything."

"I've seen enough, Eddie," Mr. Zimmermoon said sternly. "Please sit down."

Zeke turned to Eddie. "I'm really—" he started.

But Eddie cut him off. "Don't talk to me," he told Zeke.

Zeke turned to Amelia. "I couldn't help it. I—"

"Don't talk to me, either," Amelia said angrily.

Zeke didn't understand why Eddie and Amelia were so mad.

It wasn't his fault he had to sneeze.

The whole class had been *ha ha ha*-ing.

But Eddie and Amelia weren't mad at *them*.

They were only mad at Zeke.

Which didn't make any sense. Unless . . .

What if Amelia and Eddie didn't *know* Zeke was sneezing?

What if humans didn't go *ha ha ha* when they sneezed?

What if they made a completely different sneezing sound?

And what if *ha ha ha* meant something else on Earth?

Zeke was going to have to ask Zeus about that. Zeus was an expert on Earth stuff.

Maybe the cat could tell Zeke how to get his friends to *not* be mad at him, too.

Because without Eddie and Amelia to talk to, Zeke was going to be one lonely zeebop.

5

Z IS FOR WEIRD

Zeus! You gotta help me!" Zeke
shouted as he raced into his
house after school. "I have to
know if—"

Zeke stopped shouting when he
entered the living room.

His mom was wearing a lamp
shade on her head.

His dad was wearing a plastic
bucket on his head.

And they were both swinging

43

butter knives around like tiny swords.

Znort. Znort. Even though he felt rotten, Zeke let out a big, loud, zeebop laugh. He couldn't help himself. His parents looked hilarious. *Znort. Znort.*

But Zeus wasn't laughing. The cat was perched on a table. His claws were out, and he looked *mad.*

"Why are you hiding?" Zeus shouted angrily. "Are you aliens chicken?"

"They can't be chickens," Zeke's dad said. "They're too small."

Zeus grumbled something under his breath.

"What's going on?" Zeke finally asked.

"Put on a helmet!" Zeus told him. "Grab a sword!" He scratched his belly. "There they go again."

Zeke's dad picked up the couch cushion and peered underneath.

"No enemy here," he told Zeus.

Zeke's mom searched the drapes.

"The aliens aren't here, either, Zeus," she said.

"Keep looking!" Zeus ordered. He scratched his ear.

Zeke bet no other parents on Planet Earth were running around with lamp shades and buckets on their heads, searching for teeny tiny enemy aliens.

His family was so *weird*.

Zeus turned around and scratched his back against the wall.

Then he scratched at his tail.

And at his rear end.

Zeke frowned. Then he let out a big sneeze. *"Ha ha ha HAAA."*

"You're sicker than ever," his mother said. "I knew this would happen if you went to school. You need a nap!"

This time, Zeke listened to his mother.

He went upstairs to stand on his head for a while.

Zeke was feeling really lousy.

But it had nothing to do with having a cold.

And everything to do with losing his two best friends.

Being stuck on Earth with no other kids to hang out with was even worse than being sick.

ONE MEAN MACHINE

6

The next morning, as Zeke walked onto the school playground, he felt something wet drip down his cheek. It was a green tear.

He still had the zeebop flu.

Zeke probably should have stayed home and rested.

But he couldn't really get much sleep at home. Not with Zeus and his parents searching for aliens.

They had been slamming doors and

knocking things around all morning.

Hunting tiny aliens was a noisy job.

Zeke looked around the playground. There were kids everywhere.

Some kids were on the swings with their friends.

Some kids were playing tag with their friends.

Some kids were just talking to their friends.

Everyone had friends.

Except Zeke. He didn't have friends anymore.

Eddie and Amelia were sitting on a bench together. But there wasn't any room on that bench for Zeke.

"Ha ha ha." Zeke sneezed.

Then he wiped away green goo

from his eyes and his mouth. Even his eye *teeth* were tearing. This was one bad flu.

Zeke watched as Amelia reached into her backpack. She pulled out two red, sugary circles.

Zeke remembered the first time Amelia had given him one of those. It was sweet. And really, really crunchy.

Eddie had said you were supposed to lick a lollipop, not bite it. But Zeke liked when things crunched in his mouth.

Zeke sure would have loved a lollipop right now. But there was no way Amelia was giving him one of hers.

Zeke was really homesick for Planet Z. He had lots of friends there.

And they didn't get mad at him just for sneezing.

Ha ha ha. Zeke sneezed.

Suddenly Zeke heard someone shouting.

"Hey! Put me down!"

Zeke turned just in time to see Slade lifting up a smaller kid by his collar.

The kid's feet were dangling in the air. He looked a bit like Zeke did when he floated around in his family's spaceship.

Floating in space was fun.

But this kid wasn't having any fun.

He was crying. And screaming.

"Put me down!" the kid shouted again.

"Whatever you say." Slade gave the kid an evil grin. Then he let go of his collar.

Slam!

The kid landed hard. Right on his rear end.

Zeke winced. *That had to hurt.*

"That was awesome," one of Slade's friends said.

"You're one mean machine, Slade!" cheered another.

Zeke didn't understand.

Slade's friends were acting like being mean was a *good* thing.

Earth kids sure were strange.

Zeke watched as Slade and his buddies stomped over to Amelia and Eddie.

"Got any more lollipops?" Slade asked Amelia.

Amelia didn't answer. She just held her backpack a little tighter.

"Guess they're in there," Slade said. He snatched the pack out of her hands.

Amelia looked like she was going to cry.

Zeke waited for Eddie to help Amelia.

But Eddie didn't move. He just sat there. It was like he was frozen.

Zeke wanted to go over and help Amelia.

But Slade was surrounded by his big fifth-grade friends.

Those guys were mean. And strong.

There was no telling what they might do if Zeke went over to try to stop Slade from stealing Amelia's lollipops.

Unless...

What if Slade and his friends couldn't *see* him coming?

7

KITCHY KITCHY KOO

Quickly Zeke hid behind a bush.

He took off his cap.

He wiggled his right antenna.

And then he disappeared.

Well, not really. Zeke was still there. He was just invisible.

Invisible Zeke raced over to where Amelia and Eddie were sitting.

He sneaked up beside Slade. He blew hot air in his face.

"*Ewww,*" Slade said. He turned to

his pals. "Do you guys smell that?"

"Smell what?" one of Slade's friends asked.

"It kind of smells like bad breath," Slade answered.

Oops. Zeke had forgotten to brush his teeth before he left for school. His mom had been too busy looking for tiny aliens to remind him.

"Quit kidding around, Slade," another fifth-grader said. "Take the lollipops and let's get out of here."

Slade started to open Amelia's backpack.

But before Slade could grab the lollipops, Zeke reached over with his invisible fingers. He tickled Slade right on the belly.

"Hey! Cut that out!" Slade shouted.

"Cut *what* out?" one of his pals asked.

Slade looked around. "Which one of you jerks just tickled me?" he asked.

Nobody answered. They had no idea what Slade was talking about.

Zeke tickled harder. He poked Slade in his armpit.

Yuck. It was sweaty in there.

"Cut it out!" Slade shouted. He wiggled and jiggled.

The more Slade wiggled, the more Zeke tickled.

Wiggle. Jiggle.
Tickle. Tickle.

"I said stop tickling me!" Slade yelled. He was jumping all around. And then . . .

Suddenly Slade let out a loud *"ha ha ha."*

Zeke was surprised.

Was Slade sick? He didn't seem tired. His eyes weren't leaking.

But he was still *ha ha ha*-ing.

Wait a minute, Zeke thought.

Maybe Earth kids said *ha ha ha* when something felt funny.

Or when they *thought* something was funny. Like the clowns at the circus.

That was it!

Ha ha ha was the Earth way of laughing.

Just like *znort znort* was the zeebop way of laughing.

Zeke had figured it out—without Zeus's help!

No wonder Eddie was mad at Zeke. He thought he had ruined their skit on purpose.

Zeke tickled Slade again.

"Ha ha HAAAAAAAA." Slade laughed harder.

He wiggled more.

He jiggled more.

"Cut it out, Slade," one of his friends said. "People are looking at us."

"I can't stop," Slade said. *"Ha ha ha.* It tickles."

"I'm getting out of here," one of Slade's pals said. "I don't need people thinking I hang out with someone who's weird."

"I'm not weird," Slade said. "I'm just ticklish."

"What a geek," another big fifth-grader said. "Let's go, you guys."

Slade's pals walked off without him.

Now Slade was all alone. Wiggling. Jiggling. And laughing. *"Ha ha ha."*

"Wait up, you guys," Slade said. "Don't leave me here."

But Slade's friends did not wait for him.

Finally, Zeke stopped tickling Slade.

Slade stopped wiggling. He stopped jiggling. Then he looked at Amelia.

"I don't want your dumb lollipops, anyway," he told her.

Slade threw Amelia's backpack on the ground and walked away.

All alone.

Which was just what a mean kid like Slade deserved.

8

GREEN GOO—EW!

Zeke was feeling really proud of himself.

He had helped his friends.

And he had taught Slade a lesson.

Bullying is bad. It doesn't feel good when people are mean to you.

And it doesn't feel good to be all alone.

Zeke knew *he* didn't like that feeling.

He had to find a way to get Amelia

and Eddie to be his friends again . . .

But he couldn't do that if they couldn't see him.

So Zeke hurried back behind the big bush.

He wiggled his left antenna and—

Presto! Zeke wasn't invisible anymore.

He put his cap back on his head.
He took a deep breath of Earth air.
And then he bravely started walking
over to Eddie and Amelia.

"Hi, guys," Zeke said. He was trying
to sound really, really friendly.

"Hello," Amelia said.

"Hi," Eddie said.

They didn't sound really, really friendly.

But at least they were talking to him.

"I'm sorry about the skit," Zeke said. "I didn't mean to go *ha ha ha*. I couldn't help it. I . . ."

Zeke stopped. He didn't know what else to say.

"I know," Eddie interrupted him. "I kind of figured it all out."

Zeke gulped. *Uh-oh.* Had Eddie figured out that Zeke was a zeebop?

"You did?" Zeke asked nervously.

"Sure," Eddie said. "Some people laugh when they get nervous. You were just scared to do a skit in front of so many people."

Phew.

"Um . . . yeah," Zeke said. "That must have been it."

"Not everyone is cut out for showbiz like I am," Eddie continued.

"I guess not," Zeke agreed. "Anyway, I'm sorry."

Amelia smiled at him. She reached into her bag.

"You want the green lollipop?" she asked Zeke.

Zeke smiled. "Sure!" he said. "Thanks."

Zeke took the lollipop. He put it in his mouth.

He knew he should lick it, the way Earth kids did. But he couldn't help himself.

Crunch.

Chomp. Chomp. Chomp.

Amelia started laughing. *"Ha ha ha."*

Zeke knew what that meant.

"What's so funny?" he asked her.

"You've got green goo all over your lips," Amelia said. "It looks like it's dripping from your teeth."

Amelia thought the green goo

73

was from the lollipop. But Zeke knew better. The green goo was dripping from his *eye teeth*. He was still sick.

"You don't look so good," Eddie told Zeke.

"I'm not feeling very well," Zeke admitted.

"Come to think of it, you look kind of green all over," Amelia said. "Even in your eyeballs."

"That's worse than I looked when I had the flu last year," Eddie added.

"You should go to the nurse," Amelia told Zeke. "She'll call your mom and have her bring you home."

"It would feel good to go back to standing on my head for a while," Zeke agreed.

Amelia and Eddie stared at him.

Oops.

"I mean to go back to *bed* for a while," Zeke said. "I'm so sick, I don't know what I'm saying."

"Come on, we'll walk you over to the nurse," Eddie told him.

"You don't have to do that," Zeke said.

"Sure we do," Amelia said. "You look awful. You might pass out before we get to the nurse's office."

"Thanks," Zeke said as he walked into the school with Eddie and Amelia.

"No problem," Eddie told him.
"After all, what are friends for?"

Zeke smiled.

Friends.

He liked the sound of that.

BATH TIME!

But Zeke didn't like the sound of what was going on in his home later that afternoon. He was trying to nap so he could feel better.

But a kid can't nap when all he hears is—

Smack!

Crash!

It sounded like a war was going on in his living room.

Uh-oh! Had the aliens really attacked?
Quickly Zeke raced down the stairs.

His mother was in the living room,
sweeping up pieces of a broken coffee
mug. But there wasn't a tiny alien
in sight.

"*Ha ha ha.*" Zeke sneezed loudly.

His mom looked up from her sweeping and smiled at him.

"Oh, hi, honey," she said. "Are you feeling any better?"

Zeke shook his head. "It's a bad flu." He looked down at the broken cup on the floor. "What happened?"

"Zeus thought there were aliens hiding in a coffee cup," his mom answered. "He knocked it off the table when he tried to defeat them."

"Were the aliens in there?" Zeke asked.

"Nope," his mom answered. "Just some coffee grounds."

"Where's Zeus now?" Zeke wondered.

"In the kitchen with your dad," his mom answered. "Zeus thinks the aliens may be hiding in that big box that stays cold all the time. Maybe you can help them look."

But before Zeke could walk into the kitchen, there was a knock at the door.

"I'll get it," Zeke said.

He walked over and peeked out the window. Eddie and Amelia were standing on the porch.

Zeke smiled. A little green goo dripped from his eye teeth. He wiped it away and reached for the door.

"Hi," Amelia said as Zeke opened the door. "How are you feeling?"

"Still pretty rotten," Zeke admitted.

"That's a bummer," Eddie said.
He handed Zeke a folder. "This probably
won't make you feel any better."

"What is it?" Zeke asked.

"Mr. Zimmermoon asked us to
bring you your homework folder,"
Amelia told him.

"Thanks . . . I guess," Zeke said. "I—"

Before Zeke could finish his sentence, his dad came running into the living room. Mr. Zander had a bucket on his head. He was carrying a butter knife.

"I'm telling you, there's no one hiding in the cold box!"

Zeke frowned. His dad was so embarrassing.

But Amelia and Eddie didn't say a word about the way Zeke's dad looked.

Maybe Earth parents did weird things too sometimes.

A moment later, Zeus stormed into the living room.

The cat opened his mouth to say something. But he stopped when he spotted Eddie and Amelia.

"Meow," Zeus said, trying to sound like an Earth cat.

"Your kitty is so cute," Amelia said. "Can I hold him?"

"I wouldn't do that if I were you," Eddie said.

"Why not?" Amelia asked him.

"Look at him," Eddie said.

Zeke looked at Zeus. The cat was scratching at his back and behind his ear.

"It looks like your cat's got fleas," Eddie told Zeke.

"Fleas?" Zeke asked.

"Yeah," Eddie said. "You know, those little bugs that crawl all over animals and bite them? Fleas sure can make an animal itch!"

Zeke grinned. So that was it.

All this time Zeus had been hunting space aliens, but he'd really just been covered in Earth bugs.

"My dog gets fleas all the time," Eddie said.

Zeus hissed angrily.

Zeke figured he wasn't happy to know he was covered in the same bugs as a dog.

"How did you get rid of your dog's fleas?" Zeke's mom asked Eddie.

"There's only one way I know," Eddie told her. "You gotta give him a flea bath."

★   ★   ★

"Zeus, hold still!" Zeke's mother shouted as she held the cat down in the flea bath that evening. "I have to rub the soap behind your ears."

"This is so embarrassing," Zeus hissed.

Zeke let out a loud *"ha ha ha ha ha ha."*

"I guess you're still not feeling any better," Zeke's dad said to him.

Zeke smiled. Actually, he was feeling better. Much better.

Those *ha ha ha*s had nothing to do with sneezing or being sick.

They had to do with how silly Zeus looked in his bath.

Zeke was laughing at something funny.

Just like any other kid on Planet Earth.

"Ha ha ha . . . ZNORT!" Well, *almost.*